Othello,
the Moor of Venice

Published by Sweet Cherry Publishing Limited
Unit 36, Vulcan House,
Vulcan Road,
Leicester, LE5 3EF
United Kingdom

First published in the US in 2013
2020 paperback edition

2 4 6 8 10 9 7 5 3

ISBN: 978-1-78226-722-5

© Macaw Books

Othello, the Moor of Venice

Lexile® code numerical measure L = Lexile® 1160L

Guided Reading Level = T

Cover design and illustrations by Macaw Books

www.sweetcherrypublishing.com

Printed and bound in India
I.TP002

About *Shakespeare*

William Shakespeare, regarded as the greatest writer in the English language, was born in Stratford-upon-Avon in Warwickshire, England, in 1564. He was the third of eight children born to John and Mary Shakespeare.

Shakespeare was a poet, playwright and dramatist. He is often known as England's national poet and the "Bard of Avon." Thirty-eight plays, one hundred and fifty-four sonnets, two long narrative poems and several other poems are attributed to him. Shakespeare's plays have been translated into every major existent language and are performed more often than those of any other playwright.

Othello: He is a general in the Venetian army. He is a powerful figure, respected by all. He wins the heart of Desdemona because of his

virtues. But later in the play, he kills her because of his insecurities based on racial and cultural differences.

Desdemona: She is the beautiful daughter of Brabantio and wife of Othello. She appears meek, but is determined and confident.

Iago: He is an ensign to Othello and the villain of the play. He is manipulative, cunning, bold and relentless. He is motivated for several reasons to take his revenge on Othello and Cassio.

Cassio: He is second in command to Othello. He is young and good looking, but lacks military experience. Iago resents his position in the military and uses him as a pawn to take revenge on Othello.

Othello, the Moor of Venice

B rabantio was one of the
richest senators in Venice.
He had a very beautiful daughter
called Desdemona, whom all the
men of Venice were crazy about.

But Desdemona always preferred the mind over the physical attributes of men—and these qualities could only be fulfilled by a black man called Othello, the Moor of Venice. Othello was very close to Brabantio, and during the many visits he had made to the senator's house, the lovely Desdemona had fallen in love with him.

But although Othello was judged for his skin color, the truth remained that there was no other

like him in the whole of Venice.
He had proved himself over
and over again in the several
wars fought between the state of
Venice and the Turks. He had
established himself as one of the
greatest generals the Venetian
army had ever seen, and his
strategies of war spoke truly
of his intellectual acumen.

But though Brabantio was
well aware of the various good
qualities of the Moor, he was
not willing to have him as his
son-in-law. He had always hoped
that his daughter would choose
a senator or someone of nobler
rank, and definitely a white-
skinned man like himself. So

her choice of Othello had not gone down very well with him.

When the private marriage between Othello and Desdemona was made public, Brabantio was convinced that the black Moor had used witchcraft on his poor unsuspecting daughter and tricked her into falling for him. He declared that it was for this

reason that his daughter had not confided in him and had eloped with Othello.

But at that time, there was another important matter that also had to be looked into. News arrived that the Turks had once again laid

siege to the fortress of Cyprus
in a bid to take it back from the
Venetians. Othello therefore
appeared before the senate
on two counts—as a general
whose services were desperately
needed by the state, and also as a
fugitive, who had been charged

by Senator Brabantio for having abducted his innocent daughter.

Brabantio's age and seniority in the senate allowed him a hearing from the members of the senate present. But since he was so emotionally

charged when making his
accusations against Othello,
the jury could not take him
seriously. On the other hand,
Othello merely recounted how
he had won over Desdemona by
telling her tales of his conquest
and other stories whenever he
visited Brabantio's house. The
court came to the conclusion

that Othello had merely wooed
the noble Desdemona, and that
could not be labeled a crime.

But even more in Othello's
favor was the testimony of
Desdemona herself. She appeared
in court and claimed that while
she was indebted to her father
for her life and education, she
had chosen to marry Othello

of her own accord. The court
now had no doubts about the
matter and the verdict was
clearly stated in Othello's favor.

Brabantio realized there was nothing he could do but give his daughter to the Moor with his blessing. But in his state of sorrow and misery, he told Othello, "Look at her, Moor, if you have eyes to see with. She has deceived her father and she may deceive you as well." So saying, Brabantio left.

Now it was time for Othello to set sail for Cyprus to deal with matters of the state. Desdemona, not wanting to be parted from her husband so soon after their marriage, asked if she could accompany him. Othello was only too happy to agree. Upon

reaching Cyprus, they were
told that a tempest had blown
away all the Turkish fleets, and
so the city was safe from any
foreign conquest. Othello was
pleased, as now he would have
more time to spend with his new
bride. Little did he know that
the war was just about to begin.

Along with Othello, Michael
Cassio had come to Cyprus to
face the Turkish invasion. Cassio
was one of the Moor's closest
friends—a valiant Florentine,
who was adept in charming
women off their feet. Any other
man would surely be jealous
of Cassio being around his

beloved, but Othello felt no
jealousy, and had no reason to
doubt either Desdemona or
Cassio. So, when Desdemona

and Cassio spent time together, laughing at Cassio's jokes or at his various stories, Othello did not give it a passing thought.

Othello had recently promoted Cassio to lieutenant, making him second in command. This had not gone

down well with many of the
soldiers in the army, especially
Iago, a more senior officer, who
felt that the promotion should
have been given to him rather
than Cassio, a mere novice. It was
true that Iago hated Cassio, but
now he hated Othello even more.

Iago's wife, Emilia, was a maid to Desdemona and learned that Othello was madly in love with his wife. Iago then started devising a plan, which would simultaneously generate the downfall of Cassio, Othello and Desdemona.

Now Iago was a shrewd man and he knew that mental

anguish could cause a person
much more distress than
bodily torture; jealousy was
more powerful than the most

potent poison. He decided that if only he could prove to Othello that Cassio had been courting his fair wife, it might be reason enough for Othello to kill Cassio, or vice versa.

With the welcome news of the loss of the Turkish fleet, the whole island of Cyprus was

in a state of merriment.
Wine was flowing in
abundance and everyone
drank a toast to Othello
and his beautiful wife,
Desdemona. It was during
that night that Iago
decided to put his plan
into action. He had met a
man called Rodriguez on
the island, who was deeply
in love with Desdemona
and had been heartbroken
to learn of her marriage to
Othello. Iago knew that
this man would perhaps
be the best person to help
him get things started.

That night, Iago first
decided to get Cassio suitably
drunk, knowing that he could
not hold his drink. Then, Iago
encouraged Rodriguez to start
talking ill of Bianca, a woman
with whom Cassio was very
much in love. Cassio, now
considerably drunk, soon lost

control of his emotions and
became embroiled in a fight with
Rodriguez. Iago, whom Othello
had put in charge of maintaining
peace and order that night, tried
to stop them, but only managed
to spur them on further.

The ruckus brought Othello
out into the streets, and he
immediately wanted to know
who had started the brawl so that
he could mete out an appropriate
punishment to the guilty party.
But Iago, evil mastermind that
he was, tried to place all the

blame on himself, declaring to
the Moor that it was he who had
been unable to stop the fight and
so he should be punished. But
finally, when it was learned that
the guilty party was none other
than his own lieutenant, Cassio,
Othello was beside himself

with rage and at once banished him, taking back his title.

Iago kept trying to intervene, begging that Cassio be forgiven, but Othello was so livid that nothing could change his mind. But in the process, Othello's fondness for Iago grew and he

was pleased to see that Iago
had a sense of sacrifice.

Later that night, when Cassio
rued his actions before Iago, the
villain decided to take his game
to another level. He advised
Cassio that after marriage, wives
always have the upper hand over
their husbands. He therefore

told him to go and plead his
case to Desdemona, begging
her to help him get back in
favor with the general. Cassio,
thanking his esteemed friend,
decided to go to meet the noble
lady at once. Desdemona was
obviously shocked to hear
all that had happened that

night, and told Cassio that
she would definitely talk to
her husband about his case.

When the Moor returned
to his wife, she told him that
he should immediately forgive
Michael Cassio and reinstate
him to his previous rank.
Othello tried to delay the topic
to a later date, but the innocent

Desdemona would not have it. She was adamant that Othello talk to Cassio the next morning and not a minute later. Othello of course did not like this, but to keep Desdemona in good humor, he declared that he would do as she asked.

The next day, Desdemona called Cassio and explained to him what had taken place between her and Othello the night before, assuring him that he would soon find favor with the Moor again. Just as Cassio was leaving

after thanking Desdemona
for her efforts, Othello and
Iago entered the house. Upon

seeing Cassio come out of Desdemona's chambers, Iago mumbled, "I do not like that." Othello disliked what Iago was suggesting and immediately asked him the reason for his words. Iago again tried to defuse the situation by diverting the Moor's mind to other matters, but Othello would not give in.

Finally, after many excuses, Iago confessed that he did not enjoy seeing Cassio spend so much time with Desdemona. After all, the lieutenant was a young man and tales of his charm were well known in

Venice. However, he also
confirmed that Desdemona
was truly in love with her
husband and so Othello had
nothing to worry about.

Iago knew that he had sown
the seeds of jealousy in Othello's
mind. All he needed now was
some ploy by which to prove

to Othello discreetly
that Cassio was
indeed trying to woo
Desdemona, and that
his loving wife was
actually falling for
the young lieutenant.
And that chance
came rather soon.

Iago's wife,
Emilia, went to him
a few days later and showed
him a handkerchief she had
found, wondering if her husband
knew to whom it belonged. Now
Iago was a rather observant soldier
and he at once recognized it as
belonging to Desdemona. As a
matter of fact, he remembered

that it had been a special present
from Othello and that she was
dearly fond of it. So he put his
final plan into action at once.

The next day, when he met
Cassio, he tried to cheer him up
with tales of how Desdemona
would see to it that he was
back in favor with the Moor.

Cassio also tried to share his enthusiasm and hoped that things would work out for the best. Iago then urged him to spend some time with his beloved Bianca and forget about his troubles for a while. He gave him Desdemona's handkerchief and told him to give it to Bianca as

a gift, which would make her
love him even more. Cassio,
thinking that Iago was truly his
best friend in the whole world,
thanked him profusely and
set off for Bianca's quarters.

Later that day, when Iago
was alone with Othello, he tried

to talk to him about Cassio. He told Othello that the young man was most honorable and would often give his beloved Bianca gifts. Why, just the other day he had seen him give her a beautiful handkerchief, much like the one the Moor had given Desdemona.

This immediately set Othello's mind racing as he wondered how the handkerchief that his friend mentioned could be the same as the one he had given to his wife.

The Moor told Iago of his suspicions, and though Iago tried to dispel his fears at first, he mentioned how Cassio had

been showing it off as a gift
from a beautiful lady. This raised
Othello's suspicions, and he
realized that his fair Desdemona
had been seeing Cassio and
exchanging love tokens with

him. Othello wanted to murder Desdemona immediately, but Iago convinced him to first see if there was any truth in it.

So that night, Othello decided to put the question to Desdemona. Meanwhile, Iago assured Othello that he would arrange Cassio's death

and ensure that he never heard
of the vile lieutenant again.

When Othello went into
Desdemona's room that night,
he pretended to be unwell. He
asked for a handkerchief to
wipe his brow, and when she
gave him her own, he asked her
for the one that he had given

to her as a gift. She admitted
honestly that the handkerchief
was lost. But Othello then told
her that he knew she had given
it to Cassio as a token of her
love. Desdemona was distraught.
She could not believe that her
husband, the man she loved,

was accusing her of being in love with someone else.

Othello was now convinced that Desdemona was feigning ignorance and trying to divert his attention from the matter at hand. Unable to bear her dishonesty any

longer, he suffocated her
in bed with a pillow.

Emilia, who as usual had
gone to check if her mistress
needed anything before she
went to sleep, entered the room

and was the first to discover the murder. She started wailing, which alerted the guards. When they discovered the noble Desdemona dead, they were shocked when they realized

the culprit was none other than their general, the valiant Othello.

Othello lost no time in telling them what had happened over the past few days. He explained how Desdemona had been disloyal to him and that she

returned the love of Michael
Cassio. He also explained the
episode about the handkerchief,
but at this point, Emilia
interrupted. She told the people
present that she had found
the handkerchief and given it
to Iago. Othello realized that
Iago had been lying to him
about Desdemona the whole
time, and it dawned on him

that he had murdered his
innocent wife simply because
he could not keep his jealousy
in check. Unable to live with
his guilt, Othello drew his
sword and slit his own throat,
falling over the body of the
sweet Desdemona, dead.

Meanwhile, Iago had
been able to wound but not

kill Cassio, while Cassio had managed to elude the murderous Iago and drag himself, limping, to the court, followed all the way by his murderer. But as soon as Iago entered the room, the guards tried to arrest him.

Iago, looking at the people present, knew at once that his wife must have told them the story about the handkerchief. Without wasting another moment, Iago thrust his knife into his wife, killing her almost instantly. But though Emilia could not be saved, the guards arrested Iago at once. Later, he was charged with the murder of all three people—Othello, Desdemona and Emilia— and was sentenced to a most gruesome death. A fitting punishment indeed for the man who had killed the noble Othello and his treasured Desdemona.

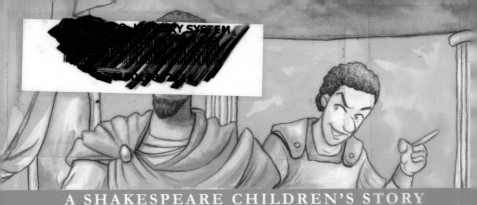

A SHAKESPEARE CHILDREN'S STORY

Othello, the Moor of Venice

Othello, the Moor of Venice is one of the most powerful tragedies by William Shakespeare. Othello is a Moorish general who falls in love with Desdemona, the daughter of a powerful senator of Venice. The play is about their love and Othello's mistrust and jealousy, which ultimately leads to a murder.

This short narrative version of the play has been suitably adapted to help introduce the play to young readers. It can be read by children or read to them by parents who wish to introduce them to the play. It can also be used by teachers as a classroom resource. The easy-to-read narration and comic-style illustrations are sure to captivate children's interest and develop their reading skills.

© Macaw Books
Written & Illustrated by:
Macaw Books

Sweet Cherry

R.R.P. $5.99 USD
ISBN 978-1-78226-722-5

9 781782 267225

Visit us at www.sweetcherrypublishing.com